Digger Pig
and the
Turnip

Digger Pig
and the
Turnip

Caron Lee Cohen

Illustrated by Christopher Denise

Green Light Readers
Harcourt, Inc.
Orlando   Austin   New York   San Diego   Toronto   London

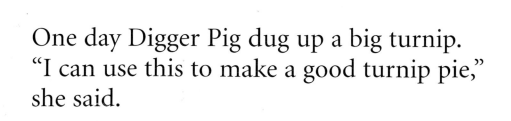

One day Digger Pig dug up a big turnip.
"I can use this to make a good turnip pie,"
she said.

Chirper Chick, Quacker Duck, and
Bow-Wow Dog sat around in their
corner of the barn.

"Let's make a turnip pie," said Digger Pig.
"Who will help me cut the turnip?"

"Not I," said Chirper Chick.
"Not I," said Quacker Duck.
"Not I," said Bow-Wow Dog.

"All right then. I will cut the turnip myself," said Digger Pig.

And she did.

Then Digger Pig asked, "Who will help me mash the turnip?"

"Not I," said Chirper Chick.
"Not I," said Quacker Duck.
"Not I," said Bow-Wow Dog.

"All right then. I will mash the turnip myself," said Digger Pig.

And she did.

Next, Digger Pig asked, "Who will help me make the pie?"

"Not I," said Chirper Chick.
"Not I," said Quacker Duck.
"Not I," said Bow-Wow Dog.

"All right then. I will make the pie myself!" said Digger Pig.

And she did.
She called her piglets to supper.

"Can we have some pie?" the others asked.

"No!" grunted Digger Pig. "You didn't help. My piglets and I will eat it all."

And they did!

Act It Out!

WHAT YOU'LL NEED

 paper

 crayons or markers

 scissors

Popsicle sticks

 tape

1. Draw Digger Pig and her friends.

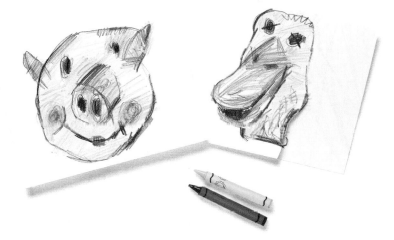

2. Cut them out.

3. Tape a Popsicle stick to each puppet.

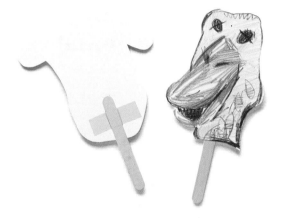

4. Think of new stories for Digger Pig and her friends.

5.

Have a Digger Pig puppet show!

Meet the Illustrator

Christopher Denise likes drawing animals. Before he starts to draw, he looks at pictures of real animals to get ideas. He says, "I know children will like a story even more if the animals are really special."

Requests for permission to make copies of any part of the work should be mailed
to the following address: Permissions Department, Harcourt, Inc.,
6277 Sea Harbor Drive, Orlando, Florida 32887-6777.

www.HarcourtBooks.com

First Green Light Readers edition 2000
Green Light Readers is a trademark of Harcourt, Inc., registered in the
United States of America and/or other jurisdictions.

The Library of Congress has cataloged an earlier edition as follows:
Cohen, Caron Lee.
Digger Pig and the turnip/Caron Lee Cohen;
illustrated by Christopher Denise.
p. cm.
"Green Light Readers."
Summary: In this adaptation of a traditional folktale,
a dog, duck, and chick refuse to help a pig prepare a
turnip pie but nevertheless expect to eat it when it's ready.
[1. Folklore.] I. Denise, Christopher, ill. II. Title.
PZ8.1.C66455Di 2000
398.24'52—dc21 99-6802
ISBN 0-15-204869-3
ISBN 0-15-204829-4 (pb)

A C E G H F D B
A C E G H F D B (pb)

Ages 5-7
Grade: 1
Guided Reading Level: F-G
Reading Recovery Level: 13-14

Green Light Readers
For the reader who's ready to GO!

"A must-have for any family with a beginning reader."—*Boston Sunday Herald*

"You can't go wrong with adding several copies of these terrific books to your beginning-to-read collection."—*School Library Journal*

"A winner for the beginner."—*Booklist*

Five Tips to Help Your Child Become a Great Reader

1. Get involved. Reading aloud to and with your child is just as important as encouraging your child to read independently.

2. Be curious. Ask questions about what your child is reading.

3. Make reading fun. Allow your child to pick books on subjects that interest her or him.

4. Words are everywhere—not just in books. Practice reading signs, packages, and cereal boxes with your child.

5. Set a good example. Make sure your child sees YOU reading.

Why Green Light Readers Is the Best Series for Your New Reader

● Created exclusively for beginning readers by some of the biggest and brightest names in children's books

● Reinforces the reading skills your child is learning in school

● Encourages children to read—and finish—books by themselves

● Offers extra enrichment through fun, age-appropriate activities unique to each story

● Incorporates characteristics of the Reading Recovery program used by educators

● Developed with Harcourt School Publishers and credentialed educational consultants

Daniel's Mystery Egg
Alma Flor Ada/G. Brian Karas

Animals on the Go
Jessica Brett/Richard Cowdrey

Marco's Run
Wesley Cartier/Reynold Ruffins

Digger Pig and the Turnip
Caron Lee Cohen/Christopher Denise

Tumbleweed Stew
Susan Stevens Crummel/Janet Stevens

The Chick That Wouldn't Hatch
Claire Daniel/Lisa Campbell Ernst

Splash!
Ariane Dewey/Jose Aruego

Get That Pest!
Erin Douglas/Wong Herbert Yee

Why the Frog Has Big Eyes
Betsy Franco/Joung Un Kim

I Wonder
Tana Hoban

A Bed Full of Cats
Holly Keller

The Fox and the Stork
Gerald McDermott

Boots for Beth
Alex Moran/Lisa Campbell Ernst

Catch Me If You Can!
Bernard Most

The Very Boastful Kangaroo
Bernard Most

Farmers Market
Carmen Parks/Edward Martinez

Shoe Town
Janet Stevens/Susan Stevens Crummel

The Enormous Turnip
Alexei Tolstoy/Scott Goto

Where Do Frogs Come From?
Alex Vern

The Purple Snerd
Rozanne Lanczak Williams/
Mary GrandPré

Look for more Green Light Readers wherever books are sold!